KT-156-087

This Book Belongs To

. . J o e . . c a s e y .
. . . .

Text copyright © 2000 Margaret Ryan
Illustrations copyright © 2000 David Melling

First published in 2000
by Hodder Children's Books

The rights of Margaret Ryan and David Melling to be
identified as the author and illustrator of this work respectively
have been asserted by them in accordance with the Copyright,
Designs and Patents Act 1988.

10   9   8   7   6   5   4

All rights reserved. No part of this publication may be
reproduced, stored in a retrieval system, or transmitted, in
any form or by any means without the prior written
permission of the publisher, nor be otherwise circulated in
any form of binding or cover other than that in which it is
published and without a similar condition being imposed
on the subsequent purchaser.

All characters in this publication are fictitious and any
resemblance to real persons, living or dead, is purely
coincidental.

A Catalogue record for this book is available from the
British Library

ISBN 0 340 77934 9

Printed and bound in Great Britain
by Omnia Books Ltd, Glasgow

Hodder Children's Books
A Division of Hodder Headline Limited
338 Euston Road, London NW1 3BH

Rainbow to the Rescue

Written by Margaret Ryan

Illustrated by David Melling

*Hodder
Children's
Books*

a division of Hodder Headline Limited

To Sheena
with love –
Margaret Ryan

For Matthew and Kelsie –
David Melling

Rainbow, the parrot, never stopped talking. She talked all day.

"Good day. Nice day. Sunny day. Holiday!"

She talked all night.

"Cold night. Dark night.
Spooky night. Goodnight!"

She even talked in her sleep.

"Who's a pretty girl, then?
I am. SNORRRRRRRRE."

Sometimes her jungle friends just wished she would be quiet.

"Can't you stop talking for *three* minutes?" said Fuzzbuzz, the little orang-utan, covering his ears with his hands.

"My ears are worn out just listening to you."

"Stop talking?" said Rainbow.

"A parrot stop talking? Don't be so silly, Fuzzbuzz. Parrots are *supposed* to talk. Don't you know anything?"

And she talked and talked and talked.

"Can't you stop talking for *two*
minutes, then?" asked Bumpy,
the sun bear, covering her ears
with her paws.

"My ears are worn out just listening to you."

"Stop talking?" said Rainbow.
"A parrot stop talking? Don't
be so silly, Bumpy. Parrots are
supposed to talk. Don't you
know anything?"
And she talked and talked
and talked.

"Can't you stop talking for *one* minute, then?" said Smiler, the crocodile, covering his ears with his claws.

"My ears are worn out just listening to you."

"Stop talking?" said Rainbow.

"A parrot stop talking? Don't be so silly, Smiler. Parrots are *supposed* to talk. Don't you know anything?"

And she talked and talked
and talked.

At last the jungle friends could
stand it no longer.

"Please stop talking, Rainbow," said Fuzzbuzz.

"Please *please* stop talking, Rainbow," said Bumpy.

"Please *please* **please** stop talking, Rainbow," said Smiler.

But Rainbow didn't listen. She just talked and talked and talked.

The jungle friends got very cross. "Oh do be quiet, Rainbow," they yelled, "and give your beak a rest."

"Well, if that's how you feel,"
sniffed Rainbow. "I'll fly off then.
I know when I'm not wanted.
I won't stay and talk if you don't
want to listen. I can take a hint.
I'm going . . ."

"Then go," yelled the
jungle friends. "Now!"

And Rainbow went. Fluttering off
through the trees. Still talking . . .

"I can take a hint.
I know when I'm not wanted.
I'm going . . . going . . . gone."

At last all was quiet.

"This is nice," said the
jungle friends.

Smiler smiled,
slid into the river
and snored gently.

Snorrrrrrrrrk
uff uff uff

Bumpy smiled,
climbed a tree,
and ate far too
much honey.

Burp! oops,
pardon!

Fuzzbuzz
smiled, climbed
another tree,
and swung
gently from
the branches.

Crick crick
creeeaaak

"It really is quiet," they all said.

27

Five minutes later . . .

"We're fed up with all this quiet. Where's Rainbow?" said the jungle friends.

"I think
we hurt her
feelings,"
said
Bumpy.

"We shouldn't
have yelled,"
said Smiler.

"Let's go
and look for
her and tell
her we're
sorry," they
all said.

First they looked for her up in
the trees.

"Rainbow, Rainbow.
Where are you?"
But Rainbow didn't reply.

"Have you seen Rainbow?"
the jungle friends asked the
monkeys. "Sometimes she flies
up here for a chat."

"Sorry," munched the monkeys.
"We've been too busy eating to
have a chat."

Next they looked for her in the bat cave.

"Rainbow, Rainbow.
Where are you?"
But Rainbow didn't reply.

"Have you seen Rainbow?"
the jungle friends asked the bats.
"Sometimes she flies in here
for a chat."

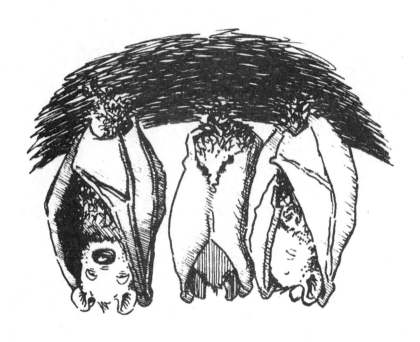

"Sorry," yawned the bats.
"We've been too busy sleeping
to have a chat."

Finally they looked for her in the bushes.

"Rainbow, Rainbow.
Where are you?"
But Rainbow didn't reply.

"Have you seen Rainbow?"
the jungle friends asked two tiger
cubs. "Sometimes she flies in here
for a chat."

"Sorry," growled the tiger cubs.
"We've been too busy playing
to have a chat."

"Where can she be?" wondered the jungle friends. "She's not in the trees. She's not in the bat cave. She's not in the bushes.

"Where CAN she be?"

"Rainbow, Rainbow. Where are you?" they called again and again. Rainbow didn't reply.

But somebody else did . . .

**"WE'RE LEAN,
WE'RE MEAN,
WE'RE VERY VERY KEEN
TO STING ANY BIT OF YOU
THAT CAN BE SEEN!"**

"Oh no," cried the jungle friends.
"It's the Angry Ant Gang."

"They're all
around us,"
cried Fuzzbuzz.

"We're going to
be stung," cried
Bumpy.

"There's no way out!"
cried Smiler.

"Yes there is," cried a voice from above. "The way to the old boat is clear. Go that way. I'll sort out the Angry Ant Gang."

"Hooray!" cried the jungle
friends. "It's Rainbow to
the rescue!"

Rainbow flew round and round and round the Angry Ant Gang.

They watched her go round and round and round till they were dizzy dizzy dizzy.

Then she began to talk to them.
She talked and talked and
talked . . .

"Hi guys," she chattered.
"Did I ever tell you about the
time I was lost in the jungle?

"I flew here and there, up and
down, round and round, but I
still couldn't find my way back to
the river.

"So I just said to myself, 'Rainbow,
what you should do is . . .'"

"What we should do is get out of here," muttered the Angry Ant Gang. "We're all dizzy and worn out just listening to her."

And they staggered off muttering . . .

"THAT BIRD BIRD BIRD IS ABSURD SURD SURD, SHOULD BE SEEN SEEN SEEN BUT NEVER HEARD HEARD HEARD."

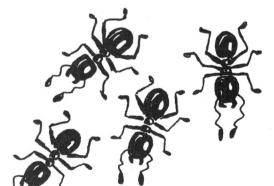

"Well done, Rainbow," cried the
jungle friends. "You've scared off
the Angry Ant Gang. We're so
sorry we were rude to you."

"That's all right," said Rainbow.
"I know I talk too much. I can't
help it. I sat in the old boat and
tried to be quiet, but I couldn't.

"Did I ever tell you about the
time I was so busy talking that
I flew CRASH BANG WALLOP
right into a tree?"
"Yes," grinned the jungle friends,
"but tell us again anyway."